Little Miss Inventor!

Mr Happy explained the problem.

"It just so happens that I have the very thing," said Little Miss Inventor. "It is my brand new shrinkometer which I invented for Mr Greedy to fit more food into his fridge, but it can shrink anything. Even people!"

They took the shrinkometer to the garden and then
Little Miss Inventor shrank Mr Happy and Little Miss Tiny.

They shrank smaller.
And smaller.
And smaller.
And smaller.

And then she shrank lots of other friends to make as large
a search party as possible.

She even shrank herself.

It was very strange being so small and the grass being so tall.

They were as small as an ant. In fact, they were smaller than an ant as they suddenly discovered!

The ant was extraordinarily strong for its size. It picked up Little Miss Bossy to take back to its anthill.

"Put me down!" ordered Little Miss Bossy, but the ant took no notice.

Fortunately, Mr Strong was even stronger than the ant.

They began their hunt for the thimble and before long came to a great mound of earth.

It was a molehill, or rather, a mole mountain.

"Maybe the thimble fell down inside the mole hill," suggested Mr Happy.

They climbed down into the mole hill, but they quickly became lost in the twisting, turning tunnel.

Luckily, they were found by a friendly
worm who showed them the way out.

As they continued their search in the garden, it began to rain, or so they thought. But it wasn't rain, it was a sprinkler.

Huge drops of water fell from above in great, wet splashes and they all huddled under the shelter of a toadstool.

"We have to turn off the sprinkler!" cried Little Miss Inventor. "Or we'll be washed away!"

"But how will we reach the tap?" exclaimed Little Miss Tiny.

It was Mr Tickle's long arm that came to their rescue.

He ran through the sprinkler drops wearing an empty snail shell on his head for protection and reached up with his long, long arms and turned off the tap.

However, their troubles were not over.

Down in the flower bed they found themselves face to face with a giant stag beetle.

It was the size of a rhinoceros!

And had a bad temper to match. It chased them up a flower.

They were stuck, with no way down.

But their escape proved easier than they might have imagined.

They were able to jump aboard a kaleidoscope of passing butterflies who flew them to safety.

And then their search led them to the garden pond, although now it was more like a vast lake.

"However will we get across?" sighed Little Miss Tiny.

"Water lilies!" cried Little Miss Inventor.

They all climbed onto a lily pad and began to paddle across the pond.

"Look at the dragonflies!" exclaimed Little Miss Sunshine. "Aren't they beautiful?"

Suddenly, a frog landed on the edge of their lily pad and bounced Mr Bounce into the air.

"Help!" he cried.

There was nothing to stop poor Mr Bounce as he bounced uncontrollably from lily pad to lily pad across the pond.

Although, this was not quite true. There was something to stop him bouncing. A sticky spider's web.

Mr Bounce had stopped bouncing, but now he rather wished he hadn't.

A huge spider stalked across the web towards him.

"Help!" cried Mr Bounce for the second time that day.

But the spider was only interested in nice, juicy flies and a rubbery Mr Bounce did not appeal.

Once they were all together again, they got back to their search. Where was Little Miss Tiny's thimble?

In the shed at the bottom of the garden they found a caterpillar. A great, big, fat, green caterpillar fast asleep. A great, big, fat, green caterpillar wearing a hat.

Or what looked like a hat, but on second inspection proved to be a thimble. Little Miss Tiny's thimble!

Very carefully, and very quietly, Mr Tickle reached out with his extraordinarily long arms and lifted the thimble without waking the caterpillar.

Quickly, they made their way back to the shrinkometer.

Suddenly, there was a loud buzzing noise.

BUUUUUUUUUUZZZZZZZZZZZ!

"Run!" cried Mr Happy.

But there was no outrunning the bee.

And then a pair of hands scooped them up out of the grass.

It was Mr Small.

A giant Mr Small!

"Well I never!" he exclaimed.

BUZZZZ!

He carried them across the lawn to the shrinkometer and enlarged them back to normal size. Everyone was very happy to have escaped the minibeasts.

And then Little Miss Curious turned up.

"Hello, everyone," she said. "Ooh, you have new invention. What does this button do?"

"Don't press that!" cried Little Miss Inventor, but it was too late.

Little Miss Tiny had grown into Little Miss Giant!

"Well," laughed Mr Happy, "At least you won't lose your thimble again."

And even Little Miss Tiny had to laugh.

"Hee! Hee! Hee!"